Phenomena

By

E. T. A. Hoffmann

British Library Cataloguing-in-Publication Data
A catalogue record for this book is available from the
British Library

E. T. A. Hoffman

Ernst Theodor Wilhelm Hoffmann was born in Königsberg, East Prussia in 1776. His family were all jurists, and during his youth he was initially encouraged to pursue a career in law. However, in his late teens Hoffman became increasingly interested in literature and philosophy, and spent much of his time reading German classicists and attending lectures by, amongst others, Immanuel Kant.

In was in his twenties, upon moving with his uncle to Berlin, that Hoffman first began to promote himself as a composer, writing an operetta called Die Maske and entering a number of playwriting competitions. Hoffman struggled to establish himself anywhere for a while, flitting between a number of cities and dodging the attentions of Napoleon's occupying troops. In 1808, while living in Bamberg, he began his job as a theatre manager and a music critic, and Hoffman's break came a year later, with the publication of Ritter Gluck. The story centred on a man who meets, or thinks he has met, a long-dead composer, and played into the 'doppelgänger' theme – at that time very popular in literature. It was shortly after this that Hoffman began to use the pseudonym E. T. A. Hoffmann, declaring the 'A' to stand for 'Amadeus', as a tribute to the great composer, Mozart.

Over the next decade, while moving between Dresden, Leipzig and Berlin, Hoffman produced a great range of both literary and musical works. Probably Hoffman's most well-known story, produced in 1816, is 'The Nutcracker and the Mouse King', due to the fact that – some seventy-six years later - it inspired Tchaikovsky's ballet The Nutcracker.

In the same vein, his story 'The Sandman' provided both the inspiration for Léo Delibes's ballet Coppélia, and the basis for a highly influential essay by Sigmund Freud, called 'The Uncanny'. (Indeed, Freud referred to Hoffman as the "unrivalled master of the uncanny in literature.")

Alcohol abuse and syphilis eventually took a great toll on Hoffman though, and – having spent the last year of his life paralysed – he died in Berlin in 1822, aged just 46. His legacy is a powerful one, however: He is seen as a pioneer of both Romanticism and fantasy literature, and his novella, Mademoiselle de Scudéri: A Tale from the Times of Louis XIV is often cited as the first ever detective story.

Phenomena

When any allusion was made to the last siege of Dresden, Anselmus turned even paler than he ordinarily was. He would fold his hands in his lap--he would gaze before him, lost in melancholy memories--he would murmur to himself,

"God of Heaven, were I to put my legs into my new riding-boots at the proper time, and run across the bridge towards Neustadt, paying no attention to burning straw, and the bursting shells, I have no doubt that this great personage and the other would, put his head out of his carriage window and say, with a polite bow, 'Come along, my good sir, without any ceremony. I have room for you.' But there was I shut up and hemmed in in the middle of the accursed Marmot's-burrow, all ramparts, embankments, trenches, star-batteries, covered ways, &c., suffering hunger and misery as much as the best of them. Didn't it come to this, that if one happened to turn over the pages of a Roux's dictionary by way of passing the time, and came upon the word 'Eat,' one's exhausted stomach cried out in utter amazement, 'Eat? Now what does that mean?' People who had once on a time been fat buttoned their skin over them, like a double-breasted coat, a natural Spencer! Oh, heavens, if only that Master of the Rolls--that Lindhorst--hadn't been there! Popowicz of course wanted to kill me, but the Dolphin sprinkled marvellous life-balsam out of its silver-blue nostrils. And Agafia!" When he spoke this name, Anselmus was wont to get up from his seat, jump just

7

a little, once, twice, three times; and then sit down again. It was always quite useless to ask him what he really meant, on the whole, by those extraordinary sayings and grimaces. He merely answered, "Can I possibly describe what happened with Popowicz and Agafia without being supposed to be out of my mind?" And every one would laugh gently, as much as to say, "Well, my good fellow, we suppose that whether or not."

One drear, cloudy October evening, Anselmus, who was understood to be somewhere a long way off--came in at the door of a friend of his. He seemed to be moved to the depths of his being, he was kindlier and tenderer than at other times--almost pathetic. His humour (often perhaps too wildly discursive, too universally antagonistic) was bowing itself, tamed and bridled, before the mighty Spirit which had possession of his inner soul. It had grown quite dark, the friend wanted to send for lights. But Anselmus, taking hold of both his arms, said: "If you would, for once, do me a real favour, don't have lights brought. Let's be content with the dim shining of that Astral lamp which is sending its glimmer from the closet there. You can do what you please--drink tea, smoke tobacco, but don't smash any cups, or throw lighted matches on to my new trousers. Either of those things would not only pain me, but would make an unnecessary noise and disturbance in the enchanted garden into which I have at last managed to get to-day, and in which I am enjoying myself to my soul's content. I shall go and lie on that sofa."

He did so. After a considerable pause, he began:

"To-morrow morning at eight o'clock it will be exactly two years since Count von der Lobau marched out from Dresden with twelve thousand men and four-and-twenty guns, to fight his way to the Meissner Hills."

"Well," said his friend, "I have been sitting here on the stretch of an expectation, almost of a devout description, thinking I was going to hear of some celestial manifestation, coming hovering out of your enchanted garden--and this is all? What interest do I take in Count von der Lobau and his expedition? And fancy you remembering that there were just twelve thousand men and four-and-twenty guns. When did military details of the sort begin to effect a lodgment in that head of yours?"

"Are those days of mystery and fatality," said Anselmus, "which we passed through so short a time ago so completely forgotten by you that you no longer recollect the manner in which the armed monster grasped us and drove us? The noli turbare no longer held in check our own exertions of force, and we would not be held in check or protected, for in every heart the demon made deep wounds, and, driven by wild torture, every hand grasped the unfamiliar sword, not for defence, no--for attack, that the hateful ignominy might be atoned for, and revenged, by Death! Even at this hour there comes upon me, in bodily form of flesh and blood, that power which was active in those days of darkness, and drove me forth from art and science into that blood-stained tumult. Was it possible, do you think, for me to go on sitting at my desk? I hurried up and down the streets, I followed the troops when they marched out, as far as I dared, merely to see with my own eyes as much as I could, and from what I Baw to gather some hope, paying no heed to the miserable, deceptive, proclamations and news 'from the seat of war.' Very good. When at length that battle of all battles was fought, when all round us every voice was shouting for joy at new-won freedom, whilst we were still lying in chains of slavery, I felt as if my heart would break. I felt as though I must gain air and freedom, for myself and all who were chained to the stake along with me, by means of some terrible deed. It may seem to you now, and with the knowledge of me which you think you possess, incredible and ludicrous; but I can assure you that I went about with the idea in my mind, the insane idea, that I would set a match to some fort which I knew the enemy had got well-stocked with powder, and blow it into the air."

The friend could not help smiling a little at the wild heroism of the unwarlike Anselmus. The latter, however, could not see this, as it was dark; and after a few moments' silence he proceeded as follows. "You have all of you often said that a peculiar planet which presides over me has a manner of bringing marvellous matters about my path on occasions of importance, matters in which people do not believe and which often seem to myself as if they proceeded out of my own inner being, although there they are, outside of me also, taking form as mystic symbols of that element of the marvellous which we find all about us everywhere in life. It was so with me this day two years ago in Dresden.

That long day had dragged itself out in dull, mysterious silence; everything was quiet outside the gate--not a shot to be heard. Late in the evening--it might have been about ten o'clock, I slunk into a coffee house in the old market, where, in an out-of-the-way back room into which none of the hated foreigners were allowed to penetrate, friends of like minds and opinions gave each other reassurance of comfort and hope. It was there where, notwithstanding all the lies which were current, the true news of the engagements at the Katzbach, Culm, &c., were first received, where our R. told us of the victory at Leipzig two days after it happened, though God knows how he obtained his knowledge of it. My way had led me past the Brühl Palace, where the Field Marshal was quartered, and I had been struck by the unusual lighting-up of the salons, as well as the stir going on all over the house. I was just mentioning this to my friends, with the remark that the enemy must have something in hand, when R. came hurrying in, breathless, and in great excitement. 'Hear the latest thing,' he began at once. 'There has been a Council of War at the Field Marshal's. General Mouton (Count von der Lobau) is going to fight his way to Meissen with twelve thousand men and four-and-twenty guns. He marches out this morning.' After a good deal of discussion we at last adopted R.'s opinion that this attack, which, from the unceasing watchfulness of our friends outside, might very probably be disastrous to the enemy, would very likely force the Field Marshal to capitulate, and so put a period to our miseries. "How," thought I, as I was going home about midnight, "can R. have found out what the decision come to was almost at the very moment it was arrived at?" However, I was presently aware of a hollow, rumbling sound making itself audible through the deathly stillness of the night. Guns and ammunition waggons, well loaded up with forage, began passing slowly by me in the direction of the Elbe bridge. "R. was right then," I had to say to myself. I followed the line of their march and got as far as the centre of the bridge, where there was at that time a broken arch, temporarily repaired with wooden beams and scaffolding. At each side of this construction was a species of fortification, constructed of high palisading and earth-works. Here, close to this fortification, I took up my position, pressing myself close to the balustrade of the bridge so as not to be seen. It now seemed to me that the tall palisades began moving backwards and forwards, and bending over towards me, murmuring hollow, unintelligible words. The deep darkness of the cloudy night prevented my seeing anything clearly; but when the troops had crossed, and all was as still as death on the bridge, I could make out that there was a deep, oppressed breathing near me, and a faint, mysterious whimpering or whining--one of the dark, scarcely distinguishable baulks of the timber was rising into a higher position. An icy horror fell upon me, and, like a man tortured in a nightmare dream, firmly fettered by leaded clamps, I could not move a muscle. The night-breeze rose, wafting mists about the hills: the moon sent feeble rays through rents in the clouds. And I saw, not far from me, the figure of a tall old man with silvery hair and a long beard. The

12

mantle which fell over his haunches he had cast across his breast in numerous heavy folds. With his long, white naked arm he was stretching a staff far out over the river. It was from him that the murmuring and whimpering proceeded. At that moment I heard the sound of marching coming from the town, and I saw the sheen of arms. The old man cowered down, and began to whimper and lament, in a pitiful voice, holding out a cap to those who were coming over the bridge, as if asking for alms. An officer, laughing, cried, "Voilà St. Pierre, qui veut pêcher!" The one who came next stopped, and said very gravely, "Eh bien! Moi, pêcheur, je lui aiderai à pêcher." Several officers and soldiers, quitting the ranks, threw the old man money, sometimes silently, sometimes with gentle sighs, like men in expectation of death; and he, then, always nodded from side to side with his head in a curious way, uttering a sort of hollow cry of a singular description. At length an officer (in whom I recognized General Mouton) came so very close to the old man that I thought his foaming charger would tramp upon him; and, turning quickly to his aide-de-camp, as he thrust his hat more firmly down on to his head, he asked him, in a loud excited voice, "Qui est cet homme?" "The escort which was in attendance on him stood motionless; but an old, bearded sapper, who was passing with his axe on his shoulder, said, calmly and gravely, "C'est un pauvre maniaque bien connû ici. On l'appelle St. Pierre Pêcheur." On that the force passed on across the bridge, not as at other times, full of foolish jesting, but in dispirited ill-temper and gloom. As the last sound of them died away, and the last gleam of their arms disappeared, the old man slowly reared himself up, and stood with uplifted head and staff outstretched, like some miraculous saint ruling the stormy water. The waves of the river rose into mightier and mightier billows, as if stirred from their depths. And I seemed to hear a hollow voice, coming up from amidst those rushing waters, and saying in the Russian language.

"Michael Popowicz! Michael Popowicz! Do you not see the fireman?"

The old man murmured to himself. He seemed to be praying. But suddenly he cried out, "Agafia!" And at that moment his face glowed in blood-red fire which seemed to be shooting up at him out of the Elbe. On the Meissner Hills great fluttering flames blazed up into the sky; their reflection shone into the river, and upon the old man's face. And now, close beside me upon the bridge, there began to be audible a sort of plashing and splashing, and I saw a dim form climbing up arduously, and presently swing itself over the balustrade with marvellous dexterity.

"Agafia?" the old man cried.

"Girl! Dorothea! In the name of heaven," I was beginning, but in an instant I felt myself clasped hold of, and forcibly drawn away. "Oh, for Christ's sake keep silence, dearest Anselmus, or you are a dead man," whispered the creature who was standing close to me, trembling and shivering with cold. Her long black hair hung down dripping, her sodden garments were clinging to her slender body. She sank down exhausted, saying, in tones of gentle complaining, "Oh, it is so cold down there! Do not say another word, Anselmus dearest, or we must certainly die."

The light of the flames was glowing upon her face, and I saw that she was Dorothea, the pretty country girl who had taken asylum with my landlord when her native village was plundered, and her father killed. He employed her as a servant, and used to say that her troubles had quite stupefied her, or otherwise she would have been a nice enough little thing. And he was right there. She scarcely spoke, except to utter a few words which sounded like incoherent nonsense, whilst her face, which would otherwise have been beautiful, was marred by a strange unmeaning smile. She used to bring my coffee into my room every morning, and I remarked that her figure, complexion, &c., were not at all those of a peasant girl. "Ah," my landlord used to say, "you see she's a farmer's daughter, and a Saxon."

As this girl was thus lying, rather than kneeling before me, half dead, dripping, I quickly pulled off my cloak and wrapped her in it, whispering to her, "Warm yourself, dear, oh, warm yourself, darling Dorothea, or you will die! What were you doing in the cold river?"

"Oh, keep silent!" she said, throwing back the hood of her mantle, and combing her dripping hair back with her fingers. "What I implore you to do is to keep silent. Come to that stone seat yonder. Father is speaking with Saint Andrew, and can't hear us."

We crept cautiously to the stone seat. Utterly carried away by the most extraordinary sensations, overmastered by fear and rapture, I clasped the creature in my arms. She sat down in my lap without hesitation, and threw her arms about my neck. I felt the icy water from her hair running down my neck; but as drops sprinkled on fire only increase its flaming, love and longing only seethed up within me the more vehemently.

"Anselmus," she whispered, "I believe you are good and true. When you sing it goes right through my heart, and you have charming ways. You won't betray me. Who would get you your coffee if you did? And, listen, when you are all starving (and you soon will be), I'll come to you at night, all alone, when nobody can know, and bake you nice cakes. I have flour, fine flour, hidden away in my little room. And we'll have bridecake, white and lovely!" At this she began to laugh, but immediately sobbed and wept. "Ah me! like those in Moskow. Oh! my Alexei! my Alexei! Beautiful dolphin, swim! Swim through the waves! Am I not waiting for you, your faithful love?" She drooped her little head, her sobs grew fainter, and she seemed to sink into a slumber, her bosom heaving and falling in sighs of longing. I looked at the old man. He was standing with outstretched arms, and saying, in hollow tones, "He gives the signal! See how he shakes his fiery locks of flame; how eagerly he treads into the ground those fiery pillars on which he traverses the land! Hear ye not his step of thunder? Feel ye not the vivifying breath which wreathes before him like a gleaming incense cloud? Hither! hither! mighty brethren!"

The sound of the old man's words was like the hollow roar

of the approaching whirlwind, and while he spoke, the fire upon the Meissner Hills blazed brighter and brighter. "Help, Saint Andrew!" the girl cried in her sleep. And suddenly she sprung up as if possessed by some terrible idea, and throwing her left arm more closely round me, whispered into my ear, "Anselmus! it would be better that I killed you," and I saw a knife gleaming in her right hand. I repulsed her in terror, with a loud cry of, "Mad creature! What would you do?" Then she screamed out, "Ah, I cannot do it! But all is over with you now!" At that moment the old man cried, "Agafia, with whom are you speaking?" And ere I could bethink me, he was close to me, aiming a stroke with his swung staff at me which would have cleft my skull in two had not Agafia seized me from behind and drawn me quickly away. The staff splintered into a thousand pieces on the stone bench. The old man fell on his knees. "Allons! allons!" resounded from all sides. I had to collect my thoughts, and spring quickly to one side to avoid being crushed by the guns and ammunition waggons which were again coming across.

Next morning the Russians drove this expeditionary force down from the hills, and back into the fortifications, notwithstanding the superiority of its numbers. "'Tis a strange thing," people said, "that our friends outside were informed of the enemy's plans, for that signal fire on the Meissner Hills had the effect of assembling the troops, so that they might make a resistance in force, just at the very time and place where he intended to concentrate his attacking bodies."

For several days Dorothea did not come in the morning

with my coffee; and my landlord, pale with terror, told me
had seen her, along with the mad beggar of the Elbe bridge,
marched off from the marshal's quarters to Neustadt under
a strong escort.

"Oh, good heavens!" said Anselmus's friend, "they were
discovered and executed."

But Anselmus gave a strange smile and said, "Agafia
got away; and, alter the Peace was signed, I received, from
her own hands, a beautiful white wedding-cake of her own
making."

The reticence of Anselmus was proof against every
effort to induce him to say anything more concerning this
astonishing affair.

When Cyprian had finished, Lothair said, "You told us
that the events which suggested this sketch would be more
interesting than it is itself; so that I consider those suggesting
circumstances are an essential part of it, without which it is
not complete. Therefore, I think you ought at once to give us
your why and wherefore, as a sort of explanatory note."

"Does it not seem to you to be as unusual as remarkable,"
said Cyprian, "that all that I have read to you is literally true,
and that even the little 'wind up,' has its kernel of actuality?"

"Let us hear!" the friends cried.

"To begin with," said Cyprian, "I must tell you that the
fate which befell Anselmus in my sketch was actually my
own, as well. My being ten minutes late decided my destiny,
so that I was shut up in Dresden just as it was surrounded on

all sides. It is a fact that after the battle of Leipzig, when our condition became more painful and trying day by day, certain friends, or mere acquaintances, whom a similar lot and a like way of thinking had drawn together, used to assemble in the back room of a coffee-house, much as the disciples did at Emmaus. The landlord, one Eichelkraut, was a reliable, trustworthy man, who made no secret of his hostility to the French, and always obliged them to treat him with proper respect and keep their due distance from him when they came in as customers. No Frenchman was allowed to make his way into that backroom on any pretext, and if one did succeed in showing his nose there, he could never get a morsel to eat, or a drop to drink, let him implore, or swear, as much as he liked. Moreover, the room was always as silent as the grave, and we all blew such stifling clouds out of our pipes that the place soon became so full of the exhalation that a Frenchman would be very soon smoked out, like a wasp, and usually went growling and swearing out of the door like one. As soon as he did, the window would be opened to let the reek out, and we would be restored to our peace and comfort again. The life and soul of those meetings was a well-known talented and charming writer: and I remember with great pleasure how he and I used to get upstairs to the upper story of the house, look out of the little garret window into the night, and see the enemy's bivouac fires shining in the sky. We used to say to each other all sorts of wonderful things which the shimmer of those fires, combined with the moonlight, used to put into our heads, and then go down and tell our friends what we imagined we had seen. It is a fact that one night one of our number (an advocate) who was always the first to hear any news, and whose reports were always reliable (heaven knows whence he derived his information), came in and told us the decision which had just been come to by the council of war concerning the expedition of Count von der Lobau, exactly as I have repeated it to you. It is likewise true that as I was going home about midnight, while the French battalions were falling-in in profound silence (no generale being beaten) and beginning their march over the bridge, I met ammunition waggons, so that I could have no doubt of the accuracy of his information. And lastly, it is the fact that, on the bridge, there was a grey old beggar lying, begging from the French troops as they crossed, whom I could not remember having seen in Dresden before. Last of all it is the fact, and the most wonderful of all, that when, much interested and excited, I reached my own quarters, on climbing up to the top story I did see a fire on the Meissner Hills, which was neither a watch fire nor a burning building. The sequel showed that the Russians must have known that night all about the attack intended to be made on the following morning, inasmuch as they concentrated troops which had been at a considerable distance upon the Meissner Hills, and it was principally Russian Landwehr which drove the French back as a storm sweeps a field of stubble. When the remnant of them fell back into the fortifications, the Russians quietly marched off to their previous positions. So that at the very time when the council of war was held at Gouvion de St. Cyr's, the decision which it arrived at was communicated to, or, more probably, overheard by persons who were not supposed to have this in their power. Strangely enough, the advocate knew every detail of the deliberation; for instance, that Gouvion was opposed to the expedition, and only yielded lest he might be thought wanting in courage, in a case where rapidity of decision was a desideratum. Count von der Lobau was determined to march out and endeavour to cut his way to the emperor's army. But how did the surrounding force know so soon of what was projected? For they knew of it in the course of an hour. Not only was it apparently impossible to get across the strongly fortified bridge; and if not, the river would have had to be swum, and the various trenches and walls got over. Moreover, the whole of Dresden was palisaded, and carefully guarded by sentries, to a considerable distance round. Where was the possibility of any human being surmounting all those obstacles in such a short space of time! One might think of telegraphic signals, made by means of lights from some tall tower or loftily situated house. But consider the difficulty of carrying that out, and the risk of detection, for such signals would have been easily seen. At all events it remains an incomprehensible thing how what actually happened came to pass; and that is enough to suggest to a lively imagination all sorts of mysterious and sufficiently extraordinary hypotheses to account for it."

"I bow my knee in deep reverence before Saint Serapion," said Lothair; "and before the most worthy of his disciples, and I am quite sure that a Serapiontic account of the important incidents of the war, as seen by him, if given in his characteristic style, would be exceedingly interesting, as well as very instructive, to imaginative members of the profession of arms. At the same time I have little doubt that the incidents in question came about quite naturally, and in the ordinary course of events. But you had to get your landlord's servant-girl, the pleasing Dorothea, into the water, as a sort of deluding Nixie; and she----"

"Don't jest about that," Cyprian said, very solemnly. "Don't make jokes on that subject, Lothair. At this moment I see that beautiful creature before my eyes, that lovely terrible mystery (I do not know what other name to call her by). It was I who had that bridecake sent to me; glittering in diamonds, flashing like lightning, wrapped in priceless sables----"

"Listen," cried Vincenz. "We are getting at it now. The Saxon maid-servant--the Russian Princess--Moskow--Dresden-- Has not Cyprian always spoken in the most mysterious language, and with the most recondite allusions, of a certain period of his life just after the first French war? It is coming out now! Speak! Let all your heart stream forth, my Cyprianic Serapion and Serpiontic Cyprian."

"And how if I keep silence?" answered Cyprian, suddenly drawing in his horns, and growing grave and gloomy. "And how if I am obliged to keep silence? And I shall keep silence!"

He spoke those words in a strangely solemn and exalted tone, leaning back in his chair, and fixing his eyes on the ceiling, as was his wont when deeply moved.

The friends looked at one another with questioning

glances.

"Well," said Lothair at last, "it seems that somehow our meeting of to-night has fallen into a strange groove of ill-fortune, and it appears to be hopeless to expect any comfort or enjoyment out of it. Suppose we have a little music, and sing some absurd stuff or other as vilely as we can."

"Yes," said Theodore, "that is the thing." And he opened the piano. "If we don't manage a canon--which, according to Junker Tobias is a thing which can reel three souls out of a weaver's body--we will make it awful enough to be worthy of Signor Capuzzi and his friends. Suppose we sing an Italian Terzetto buffo out of our own heads. I'll be the prima donna, and begin. Ottmar will be the lover, and Lothair had better be the comic old man, and come in, raging and swearing in rapid notes."

"But the words, the words," said Ottmar.

"Sing whatever you please," said Theodore; "Oh Dio! Addio! Lasciami mia Vita."

"No, no," cried Vincenz. "If you won't let me take part in your singing--although I feel that I possess a wonderful talent for it, which only wants the voice of a Catalani to produce itself in the work-a-day world with drastic effect, allow me at least to be your librettist--your poet-laureate. And here I hand you your libretto at once."

He had found on Theodore's writing-table the 'Indice de Teatrali Spettacoli' for 1791, and this he handed to Theodore. This indice, like all which appear yearly in Italy, merely contained a list of the titles of the operas performed, with the names of their composers, and of the singers, scene-painters, &c., concerned in their production. They opened the page which related to the opera in Milan, and it was decided that the prima donna should sing the names of the lover-tenors (with a due interspersing of Ah Dio's and Oh Cielo's), that the lover-tenor should sing the names of the prima donnas in like manner, and that the comic old man should come in, in his furious wrath, with the titles of the operas which had been given and an occasional burst of invective, appropriate to his character.

Theodore played a ritornello of the cut and pattern which occurs by the hundred in the opera buffas of the Italians, and then began to sing in sweet, tender strains "Lorenzo Coleoni! Gaspare Rossari! Oh Dio! Giuseppo Marelli! Francesco Sedini!" &c. Ottmar followed with "Giuditta Paracca! Teresa Ravini! Giovanna Velata--Oh Dio!" &c. And Lothair burst duly in with rapid, angry quavers: "Le Gare Generose, del Maestro Paesiello--Che vedo? La Donna di Spirito, del Maestro Mariella. Briconaccio! Piro, Re di Epiro! Maledetti!--del Maestro Zingarelli," &c.

This singing, which Lothair and Ottmar accompanied with appropriate gesticulations (Vincenz illustrating Theodore's impersonations with the most preposterous grimaces imaginable), warmed up the friends more and more. In a comic description of enthusiastic inspiration each seized the drift of the other's ideas. All the passages, imitations, &c. (to use musical expressions), usually employed in compositions of this description, were reproduced with the utmost accuracy--so that any one who had come in by accident would never have dreamt that this performance was improvised on the spur of the moment, even if the strange hotch-potch of names had struck him as curious.

Louder and more unrestrainedly raged this outbreak of Italian rabbia, until (as may be supposed), it culminated in a wild, universal burst of laughter, in which even Cyprian joined.

At their parting, on this evening, the friends were in a condition of wild enjoyment, rather than (as was the case on other occasions), lull of rational delight.

SECTION EIGHT.

The Serapion Brethren had assembled for another meeting.

"I must be greatly mistaken," said Lothair, "and be anything but the possessor of a native genius (supplemented by assiduous practice) for physiognomy--such as I believe that I do possess, if I do not read very distinctly in the face of every one of us (not excepting my own, which I see magically gleaming at me in yonder mirror), that our minds are all fully charged with matter of importance, and only waiting for the word of command to fire it off. I am rather afraid that more than one of us may have got shut up in one or other of his productions one of those eccentric little firework devils which may come fizzling out, dart backwards and forwards about the room, banging and jumping, and not manage to pop out of the window until it has managed to give us all a good singeing. I even dread a continuation of our last conversation, and may Saint Serapion avert that from us! But lest we should fall immediately into those wild, seething waters, and that we may commence our meeting in a duly calm and rational frame of mind, I move that Sylvester begins by reading to us that story which we could not hear on the last occasion because there was no time left."

This proposal was unanimously agreed to.

"The woof which I have spun," said Sylvester, producing a manuscript, "is composed of many threads, of the most various shades, and the question in my mind is whether--on

26

the whole--you will think it has proper colour and keeping. It was my idea that I should, perhaps, put some flesh and blood into what I must admit, is a rather feeble body, by contributing to it something out of a great, mysterious period--to which it really does but serve as a sort of framework."

Sylvester read:--

www.ingramcontent.com/pod-product-compliance
Lightning Source LLC
Chambersburg PA
CBHW021942170626
46808CB00004B/1481